OKOMI
Wakes Up Early

Helen and
Clive Dorman

Illustrated by
Tony Hutchings

Dawn Publications
in association with The Jane Goodall Institute

The sun had only just begun
to rise in the sky.

It was the start of another
hot day in the forest.

High up in the tree-tops
something was moving.

It was Okomi.

Okomi woke up very early.

He was feeling excited and
ready to start the day.

Poor Mama Du did not want
to wake up, but Okomi kept
fidgeting and wriggling
beside her.

Slowly Mama Du sat up.

She stretched, yawned
and climbed down from
her comfy nest.

Okomi leapt onto a nearby branch
and swung noisily to the ground,
hooting as he went.

Each morning Mama Du would
take Okomi off into the forest
to forage for breakfast.

He loved these walks.

Mama Du put Okomi
onto her back, ready to set off
and find some food.

As they walked through
the forest Okomi saw
a branch above him.

He was feeling playful and
grabbed it.

Okomi swung from Mama Du's
back. She tried to pull him free,
but he would not let go.

Mama Du pulled one way...

Okomi hung on!

Mama Du tried again.

This time she pulled Okomi free
and put him onto her back.

They had only taken a few steps
when Okomi leapt down to run
back and play.

Once again, Mama Du grabbed
Okomi and dragged him
after her.

Okomi thought this was
a great game!

He soon escaped again to
swing on another branch.

Then Okomi ran off
around a tree.

Although Mama Du was hungry
she knew Okomi was
too playful to want to eat.

So she laughed and chased
after him.

When Okomi saw his mommy
coming towards him
he rolled away.

She tried to grab him
but missed.

Okomi liked this game!

Mama Du tried again.

This time she grabbed
Okomi's hand and pulled him
towards her.

Okomi was so excited he nipped
her hand. Right away, Mama Du
scooped him up and gave him a
great big hug.

Then Mama Du gently tickled
him and Okomi laughed.

Mama Du cuddled Okomi
until he was calm.

Once more she put Okomi
onto her back.

But this time, tired and
hungry, Okomi stayed there.

Have a good breakfast Okomi!

Did you know?

Chimpanzees love to hug and kiss their friends and family. There are close bonds between family members. They are very intelligent.

When they are very young, baby chimpanzees cling to their mother's tummy. When they are about six months old, baby chimpanzees start to ride on their mother's back. At about the same age they start learning to walk and to climb trees.

Young chimps remain with their mothers until they are seven or eight years old. Chimpanzees in the wild can live for as long as 50 years.

Chimpanzees are our closest living relatives in the animal kingdom. These apes are found in the wild only in Africa. They share over 98% of their genetic material with us; they use and make tools; they express many of the same emotions that we do.

Fanni and her baby, Fax

Helping orphaned chimps

Jane with an orphan chimpanzee

Sadly, chimpanzee numbers are falling as their forests are cut down and they are hunted for the commercial bushmeat trade. This leaves hundreds of orphan chimps. An orphan chimpanzee can almost never be returned to the wild. Proceeds from the sale of each Okomi book supports the Tchimpounga sanctuary (in the Republic of Congo), where there are currently over 100 orphan chimps.

Roots & Shoots

One day in 1991, 16 students gathered on Dr. Jane Goodall's front porch in Dar es Salaam, Tanzania. They were fascinated by animal behavior and environmental concerns, but none of their classes covered these topics. They wanted to know how to help chimpanzees and other animals. Those 16 students went back to their schools to form clubs with other interested young people, and Roots & Shoots began. Since then, the program has spread rapidly throughout the world. More than 3,000 Roots & Shoots groups for children pre-K and up have formed in more than 68 countries around the world. There are many active groups in the U.S. and Canada.

Their mission is to foster respect and compassion for all living things, to promote understanding of all cultures and beliefs and to inspire each individual to take action to make the world a better place for the environment, animals and the human community. For more information contact the Jane Goodall Institute, P.O. Box 14890, Silver Spring, MD 20910, or call (301) 565-0086, or go to www.janegoodall.org.

Dawn Publications is dedicated to inspiring in children a deeper understanding and appreciation for all life on Earth. To view our full list of titles, or to order, please visit our web site at www.dawnpub.com, or call 800-545-7475.